Who me...
Yes me

Who me...
Yes me

J L Seawright

Copyright © J L Seawright.

All rights reserved. No part of this book may be reproduced in any form or by any electronic or mechanical means, including information storage and retrieval systems, without permission in writing from the publisher, except by reviewers, who may quote brief passages in a review.

ISBN: 978-1-64921-214-6 (Paperback Edition)
ISBN: 978-1-64921-215-3 (Hardcover Edition)
ISBN: 978-1-64945-389-1 (E-book Edition)

Some characters and events in this book are fictitious. Any similarity to real persons, living or dead, is coincidental and not intended by the author.

Sponsored by Joe LouiS Travel---Travel with a punch and JLSproductionz and Nitrojada1

Information about sheet music or recordings of the song "HEY WORLD" heard played and sung throughout the play may be obtained through georgesavan724@gmail.com.

Book Ordering Information

Phone Number: 347-901-4929 or 347-901-4920
Email: info@globalsummithouse.com
Global Summit House
www.globalsummithouse.com

Printed in the United States of America

CONTENTS

WHO ME----YES ME vii
CAST OF CHARACTERS ix
PRODUCTION NOTES xi

ACT ONE, Scene 1 1
ACT ONE, Scene 2 4
ACT ONE, Scene 3 6
ACT ONE, Scene 4 12
ACT TWO, Scene 1 17
ACT TWO, Scene 2 20
ACT TWO, Scene 3 24
ACT THREE, Scene 1, Part One 26

INTERMISSION

ACT THREE, Scene 1, Part Two 45
ACT THREE, Scene 2 72
ACT THREE, Scene 3 74
ACT THREE, Scene 3 76

EPILOGUE 81

WHO ME----YES ME

What you are about to read is a short play that is 90% fact and 10% fiction.

It is the life story of a Transsexual (LGBTQ) person, and this play details the trials and tribulations that persons of this persuasion, this identity, must contend with, from childhood through adulthood, because they are condemned by society for being "different."

This play is dedicated to my cousin Clarice, who introduced me to a doctor who performed sex reassignment surgery. That doctor allowed me to videotape five sex-change operations, over a two-day period. One month later, I videotaped three of his patients when they came in for their first office visits (post-op checkups).

Three months after that, I was permitted to follow up with two of his patients, once every three months, for nearly a year and a half.

Following that period of time, one patient dropped out, while the other one kept in touch, by phone, for nearly eleven years, and she kept me abreast of the many things that happened to her as she tried to transition into society as a full-fledged woman.

-----This is her story-----

Names have been changed to protect the guilty, along with the private and the humble.

J. L. Seawright

CAST OF CHARACTERS

SONYA	A beautiful woman in her twenties, lead character
LOLITA	An unfaithful wife
MAN	Lolita's lover
RICHARD	Lolita's son, a seven-year-old boy
JERRY	Lolita's husband, Richard's father
DEBBIE	Sonya's neighbor, best friend, and boss
RICHARD SANTIAGO MILLER	Policeman, 27, male lead character with flaws
MR. JACKSON (HENRY)	Sonya's father – stubborn, but changing his attitude
MRS. JACKSON (MARIA)	Sonya's mother – shows unconditional love
DR. KELLY	Just starting medical practice at beginning of play
NURSE JOHNSON	Very attentive and caring
ORDERLY	A large male
JOE THE COP	Eighteen years on the police force
ROOKIE COP	Four months on the job, female
DETECTIVE #1	Stern, no nonsense
DETECTIVE #2 (BEN)	Makes wise-guy statements

JUDGE FAIRCHILD	Stern, fair, and curious
DEFENSE ATTORNEY	Displays loyalty to his client
PROSECUTING ATTORNEY	Female, tough as nails
BAILIFF	A no-nonsense type
MAN IN AUDIENCE	Reading a newspaper
DR. RODRIGUEZ	30 years as a physician
DR. SUSSMAN	Brilliant psychiatrist
MR. KINGSLEY	A loving father
NURSE	Sonya's attendant in court
COURT STENOGRAPHER	Middle-aged female
JURY FOREMAN	
Group of Children	Heard playing outside Sonya's apartment window

Sonya's neighbors
Apartment building superintendent
Three uniformed policemen
Two or more court guards
Courtroom audience
Jurors
Cab driver(s)

PRODUCTION NOTES

For most of the action, the stage is divided into three sections or rooms, separate areas at stage left, center, and right that can be lighted or darkened as scenes shift. At some points there are interludes—flashbacks that may take place in one of the rooms. At other points there are back projections, filmed/videotaped actions projected on a screen as onstage action is paused.

ACT ONE

As curtain rises, "Hey WorlD" is playing

Scene 1

A couch, stage left

Lights come up slowly, revealing a man and a woman sitting on a couch, engaged in heavy petting.

Enter JERRY and his 7-year-old son, RICHARD.

JERRY *(irate)* What the hell?

LOLITA *(surprised)* It's my husband!

JERRY rushes toward the strange man and LOLITA on the couch, cursing and gesturing as he approaches.

The strange MAN jumps to his feet and dashes toward the door, pushing the little boy aside.

JERRY takes a swing at the MAN. Missing him, he focuses on his wife.

He reaches out and grabs LOLITA by her hair, throws her on the floor, kneels on her back, applying his full weight, and pulling her hair very roughly.

JERRY *(irate, yelling at his son)* RICHARD! YOU CAN'T TRUST THEM…
YOU CAN'T TRUST THEM!
Never forget that, son.
No matter how hard you work and save, sweat and give, they never appreciate you.
Now, you watch me give her what she deserves!

He begins to pummel his wife.

RICHARD goes over and tries to stop his father by grabbing his leg.

RICHARD Daddy! NO!! Don't hit my mother!

JERRY *(turns and pushes RICHARD away, yelling)* What's the matter with you, boy? Don't you understand that she's getting what she deserves?
She's been unfaithful to me and you, and if you don't help me beat her, then I'm going to beat you as well as her.
Come on, son, help me beat her or else…..!

JERRY grabs his son by his arm and pulls him toward his still pinned and screaming mother.

RICHARD balks, then reluctantly begins hitting his mother.

| **JERRY** | Hit her, hit her again, again – that's my boy!!
YOU CAN'T TRUST THEM!!
YOU CAN'T TRUST THEM! |

Stage fades to black

End of Scene 1

ACT ONE

Scene 2

A hospital birthing room, stage right

An extremely low and slow light comes up, getting wider and brighter

Voices can be heard. Sounds of birth-giving, with encouragement by those in attendance.

DOCTOR KELLY Mrs. Jackson, you've got to help us! You've got to breathe deeply and push.
It's almost over; please try just a little harder.

NURSE JOHNSON Mr. Jackson! Mr. Jackson!!
You are supposed to be helping her.

MR. JACKSON Huh.
Oh, yes – sure, I'm sorry.

He steps toward the bed where his wife is giving birth.
  Come on, honey, breathe deep and push hard.

The lights begin to fade, and as they do, the crying of a newborn child is heard.

Soft music – "Hey World" – playing as lights fade and curtain falls

End of Scene 2

ACT ONE

Scene 3

A small apartment in Greenwich Village

Sound of a telephone ringing

SONYA enters stage left, walks across the living room, which is sparsely decorated and contains two wicker chairs and a white sofa placed center stage.

She is wearing a nightgown, and she yawns as she crosses the stage toward the apartment window and raises the blinds.

It's 4 p.m. Voices of children playing in the street just below Sonya's window can be heard.

One of them looks up, sees Sonya at her window, and waves, saying "Hello." The other children join in, all are happy to see her.

SONYA *(responds to the children joyfully, trying at first to say each of their names)*
         Hi Rodney, Jackie, Todd, Nickie,
         Danielle, Jennifer, Jamillah!
         Hey Raymond and.......

| | Oh, hello to everyone! What's |
| (resolving to just say) | happening, everybody? |

She closes the window, and the children resume their play.

She walks to the center of the living room and sits on the white couch. She begins to yawn, then reaches for a photo album that is on the end table.

As she picks up the album, a photo of a little boy falls out. She picks up the photo and starts to place it in the album, then begins to daydream.

Interlude
DREAM SCENE

Stage right, in a smoky haze
A little boy is seen sitting in a living room chair playing with a GI-JOE doll. Suddenly, the child's father jerks the little boy out of the chair, shoves him toward the window, and begins to scold him for playing with the doll.

The haze begins to fade
The child runs to his mother. His mother holds him to her bosom, and they stare at the father.

There's a knock on SONYA'S apartment door at stage left, and she comes back to reality

She quickly places the photo of the little boy back in the album, next to a picture of herself. She closes the album and places it under a couch pillow before she rises and goes to the door.

She sees that it's her neighbor, DEBBIE, and she lets out a sigh of relief as she opens the door.

SONYA   Hi, Debbie, come on in. I thought you were Richard.

DEBBIE *(walks in)*   Richard? No way. I just came by for a joint. I'm on my way to work. Didn't you tell me it was over between you and that dude?

(She flops on the couch, takes a joint from her purse, and lights it.)

SONYA *(closes the door)*   Yeah, I tried. Believe me, I tried. But he doesn't want to hear it. I don't know what to do.
(Walks to the couch and sits down.)

                                       You know, even when we're out walking, he always makes such negative remarks about a lot of the women we pass in the street.

(looks at Debbie)   But still, sometimes he makes me feel so special that it scares me.

DEBBIE   That does seem weird, Sonya.

(She sits up and takes another drag, offers the joint to Sonya.)

SONYA *gestures "no" with her hands, stands and walks to a chair at stage left.*

SONYA   But tonight will be our last date – my mind is made up.

DEBBIE *(stands, walks to door)*   Well, for your sake, I hope you can get it together and make a clean split.

(pauses)   Oh, by the way, did you hear from your Pops today?

(smiles and reaches for the door)   Did he call you again?

SONYA

(goes back to the couch and sits)

Yeah, he called. That's what woke me up. I didn't answer his call Now that he knows what it's like to be near death with a bad heart, he wants me to forgive him for the way he's treated me all of my life..

DEBBIE

Are you going to?

DEBBIE opens door with a broad smile. Not waiting for an answer, she exits the apartment, leaving the door open, walks down the hallway.

SONYA
(gets off couch, walks to the door, speaks) Are you kidding – after all these years?

Not looking outside, SONYA pushes the door and turns away. A foot keeps the door from closing.
Not hearing the door close, SONYA turns and sees RICHARD.

RICHARD

Aren't you going to let me in?

SONYA *(surprised)*

Oh Richard… You're early!

RICHARD goes to SONYA, caresses her hair and kisses her gently on the cheek. Tries to kiss her again.

SONYA
(a little flustered, turns her head)

Hey, you're going to mess up my hair. Not now. Later, OK?

RICHARD
(frustrated, waving his hands and arms) Later, later, always later! OK, but get ready to go. I managed to get some tickets to a show.

SONYA | Oh, I'll be ready in a few minutes.
(turns and exits through door stage left.) | Fix yourself a drink and relax while I get it together.

(sound of a door closing)

RICHARD removes his jacket, revealing a gun. He walks to the couch, sits and leans back, looks around, sights the bar. Gets up and walks to it and starts to fix himself a drink. The sound of running water in the background.

SONYA *(from behind closed door)* | What are we going to see, Richard?

RICHARD *(still fixing his drink)* | What did you say?

SONYA *(louder; sound of water stops)* | I said, What are we going to see?

RICHARD | Well, the tickets I have say THE WIZZ.

SONYA *(excited)* | THE WIZZ!!! I've been dying to see that play. I heard it was out-a-sight! How did you get tickets?

RICHARD | Well, you know – I have connections, like my Captain.

He takes a sip of his drink, walks back to the couch, moves a pillow, and sees the photo album.
He picks it up, sits down, and starts to look through it. He sees the picture of Sonya sticking out of the back portion, pulls it out, looks at it, smiles, puts the photo in his shirt pocket.

SONYA *(enters the living room, is putting on her coat, head down)* | Well, I'm rea…

(She raises her head and sees Richard looking through the album. Excited and angry, she yells at the top of her lungs)   What the hell – Richard!!

RICHARD, startled, looks up surprised and slams the album closed.

SONYA *(just plain mad)*   What are you doing looking at those pictures?

She goes over and snatches the album away. Then she realizes what she has done and gets a grip on herself and nervously apologizes.

SONYA   I'm sorry, Richard, but these are pictures of … my … my little brother. He died a year ago. We were very, very close, and I …

RICHARD *(interrupts her)*   Hey! Don't say another word. It's me who should be apologizing, not you. … I'm sorry, I didn't know. I am sorry.

SONYA   Thank you for being so understanding.

(Relieved, she places the album on the coffee table and starts to stand erect.)

RICHARD *(takes her by the arm)*   Say, let's not spoil things for ourselves. I'll forget if you will – deal?

SONYA *(smiling)*   Deal!

RICHARD   Hey, let's not keep THE WIZZ waiting.

They pause, embrace, then clasp arms and walk toward the door.

End of Scene 3

ACT ONE

Scene 4

Interlude – on the town
BACK PROJECTION

We see shots of downtown NYC, 42nd Street and the like. THE WIZZ theater, SONYA and RICHARD, walking to his car, getting into the car. They stop at a bar. Coming out of the bar, embracing in front of Sonya's house, laughing and feeling no pain, at Sonya's apartment door.

MUSIC FROM THE WIZZ IS PLAYING LOUDLY THROUGHOUT

Back at Sonya's apartment

The scene opens with SONYA inebriated, outside her apartment door, fumbling in her purse for her keys. RICHARD is also inebriated. Their voices and sounds of their actions are heard through the door.

RICHARD takes her purse and dumps its contents on the floor in the hall. Clattering of cosmetics, keys, etc., is heard.

SONYA What are you doing?

SONYA You dumped everything out!

RICHARD That's the quickest way, baby.

They both laugh, SONYA bends over a bit unsteadily, picks up her keys and starts to pick up the rest of the articles from her purse, giggling all the time. She picks up a card; RICHARD takes it and looks at it, putting it in his pocket.

RICHARD *(shouts)* No, just the keys, baby, just the keys

Then he remembers where they are and makes hushing sounds. A jingle of keys, clumsily handled, is heard, then sounds of the door unlocking. He enters the apartment.

RICHARD *(fumbles for light switch)* Didn't you tell me that you hadn't made love since your brother died, over a year ago? Well, baby, the time has come. I know you're in the mood for me to make love to you now. Come on, honey, we'll get this stuff later. Come on, sugar, let's get it on.

SONYA *(still standing in hallway)* I hope you won't regret this.

RICHARD Regret it … no way!!

He gently pulls SONYA inside and embraces her, dragging the contents of her purse into the apartment with his foot.

SONYA reaches over Richard's shoulder and pushes the door closed. Not wasting any time, RICHARD removes his jacket and drops it on the floor. Then he removes SONYA's coat and throws it on the couch.

They move stage left, giggling and removing article after article.

They go into the bedroom, leaving the door halfway open. There's more giggling by the two of them, which slowly turns into the sounds of foreplay.

The sounds of love that emanate pause briefly, then abruptly change to sounds of hate and rage.
There's cursing, crying, yelling, fight noises, and screams of terror from SONYA.

DEBBIE *(outside door, knocking)*   Sonya, are you all right?
(She knocks harder, terrified)   Is everything all right in there?

Other NEIGHBORS start to assemble in the hall.

DEBBIE tells one neighbor to call the cops and get the super.

RICHARD rushes out of the bedroom into the living room. He hurriedly gathers his clothes together and dresses as quickly as he can. In his rush, his car keys drop out of his pocket. He's partially out of the living room window when the SUPER opens the door to allow two COPS, a veteran and a rookie, to enter the apartment. DEBBIE follows the two cops into the apartment.

ROOKIE COP *(draws her gun)*   Freeze, son-of-a-bitch, or I'll bury you right there.

RICHARD hesitates, then decides to take a chance. He exits through the window.

ROOKIE COP fires a warning shot into the ceiling.

COP JOE *(shouts at ROOKIE)*   What the hell are you doing?!

(shouts to ROOKIE, grabs his radio)   WHICH WAY IS HE GOING?,

ROOKIE   He's on West 8th Street, going east.

COP JOE   Thanks. Now, Get back, keep everyone out of here, and don't touch anything!

He speaks into his radio   Suspect is on foot, going east on West 8th toward Washington Square Park.

COP JOE rushes into the hallway, through the crowd, in pursuit of RICHARD.

Sirens are heard as backup police respond to his call.

DEBBIE *(slowly approaches the bedroom and screams)* OH MY GOD!

DEBBIE bursts into tears and very slowly backs away, goes down on both knees, and starts to sing "HEY WORLD"

The ROOKIE pushes neighbors out, closes the door, stands and watches DEBBIE.

DEBBIE slowly enters the bedroom, cringes at what she sees. Her good friend SONYA is lying in a pool of blood, motionless, looking like a battered corpse.

The ROOKIE goes over and checks Sonya for vital signs. She turns to DEBBIE.

ROOKIE Hey, she's still alive. I'm serious. She's in a bad way, but she's still alive.

DEBBIE and the ROOKIE embrace.

"HEY WORLD" music is heard……lights dim…….scene switches to street and back projection chase scene

CHASE SCENE

RICHARD approaches his car, looks for his keys, looks up, sees COP JOE, who sees him.

RICHARD turns and starts to run.

BACK PROJECTION – CHASE SCENE AND CAPTURE

RICHARD One of you got a cigarette?

DETECTIVE #1 Yeah, sure, Richard, as soon as you give us some answers.

RICHARD I already told you two, I ain't talking to nobody until I hear from the Captain.

BEN *(big smile)* Do you really think the Captain will let you continue to wear your tin till this case is investigated? No way, no way.

RICHARD What the hell you smiling about, Ben? You'd've done the same thing if you were in my shoes.

BEN Done what? You admittin' that you beat that poor girl up? Huh? Come on, spit it out, bad cop.

RICHARD *(irate, jumps to his feet)* Bad cop!! Bad Cop?!!! I'm a better cop than you'll ever be, and don't you ever forget it!!

DETECTIVE #1 Sit down, punk, you got no more privileges around here. If that girl dies, … yo' ass in grass.

BEN And I'm the lawn mower!

(The phone rings. BEN picks it up.) Interrogation.

(pause) OK, Captain!!

(hangs up the phone, looks at RICHARD)

RICHARD Well, well …? What'd he say?

BEN says nothing, just extends his hand, thumb down.

RICHARD *(slouches back in his seat)* I guess I'm ready for that cigarette now.

DETECTIVE #1 You mean you're ready to talk?

RICHARD *(dejected and defeated)* Yeah….

BEN The tin, civilian. Give me the tin.

Richard reaches into his shirt pocket and pulls out his shield. To his surprise, the picture of SONYA comes out also.

DETECTIVE #1 Is that her? Is that how she looked before you…?

(takes picture and shows it to BEN) She's a good looker, ain't she?

BEN She was…

The lights quickly go out, stage right, and slowly come up, stage left.

End of Scene 1

ACT TWO

Scene 2

HOSPITAL SCENE (center stage)

SONYA is seen with her head and hands heavily bandaged, asleep. A nurse is standing beside her hospital bed, inside the curtain that surrounds the bed.

Sonya's mother, father, and her doctor are standing at the foot of her bed outside the drawn curtain. The doctor is holding a chart and explaining Sonya's condition.

SONYA slowly blinks her eyes. NURSE JOHNSON, seeing this, calls the doctor.

NURSE JOHNSON Dr. Kelly, she's coming around. Should I give her another shot?

DR. KELLY Not yet. Let me check her vitals first.

He uses a hand signal to tell mom and pop to stay where they are, then walks toward SONYA, checks her eyes and pulse.

DR. KELLY Nurse Johnson, would you help me turn her on her side?

NURSE JOHNSON　　　　　　　　Yes, Doctor
(She walks around to the other side of the bed.)

While the doctor and nurse turn SONYA and check her, Sonya's father peers through the clear window in the curtain. MR. JACKSON now looks old and drawn. A bald spot peeks through his otherwise completely gray hair. He is slightly stooped and using a cane. Still standing outside the curtain, he turns to his wife.

MR. JACKSON　　　　　　　　Honey, if our child pulls through this, I'm going to beg her to forgive me for being such a bull-headed son of a bitch. All she ever wanted from me was a little attention. She never even asked for love, just a little attention.

MRS. JACKSON now looks slightly gray and just a bit heavier, but still has a beautiful face that is free of wrinkles.

MRS. JACKSON *(angry)*　　　　Don't you think it's too late for you to change your feelings? You should have learned to forgive and forget years ago. She's already told me that she doesn't ever want to see or speak to you again. It would take a miracle for her to forgive you after the way you treated her. Even when she was a child, you were never a real father to her.

MR. JACKSON　　　　　　　　And you know why – don't you?

The doctor and the nurse complete checking SONYA, and the doctor approaches her mother and father.

DR. KELLY　　　　　　　　　Mr. and Mrs. Jackson, she's coming around. Would you like to see her?

All three move inside the curtain to the head of the bed. But MRS. JACKSON stops, turns, and puts her hand on MR. JACKSON's chest to stop his progress.

MRS. JACKSON *(to her husband)* Henry, please…. Let me see her first.

MR. JACKSON *(dejected)* OK….OK!!

MRS. JACKSON approaches SONYA. Sonya's eyes opening slowly, she sees images around her bed staring down at her. She blinks, slowly. Her eyes clear as she looks at the familiar faces.

DR. KELLY Sonya, you're in the hospital. You have a concussion and multiple bruises, but you'll be just fine in a couple of weeks.

SONYA nods her head gently. Her eyes move on until she sees her mother's tearful eyes and sad face. She smiles – painfully.

MRS. JACKSON reaches out her hand and takes Sonya's hand and pats it gently – they both smile.

Unknown to his wife, MR. JACKSON moves closer to Sonya.

SONYA sees him, and her expression changes rapidly from a broad smile to a look of fear and anger. She releases her mother's hand.

MR. JACKSON Now, now, child, things are going to be different between us from now on.

MR. JACKSON touches her hand and she moves it out of his reach.

MRS. JACKSON and DR. KELLY step back.

NURSE JOHNSON is still on the opposite side of the bed, watching very carefully.

MR. JACKSON extends his hand to Sonya's face – her eyes begin to bulge as she recoils, pressing her head into her pillow.

SONYA *(yells, glaring at her father)* Don't touch me... DON'T TOUCH ME!

She starts to tremble from head to foot, then falls into unconsciousness.

MR. JACKSON grabs Sonya by her shoulders and lifts her slightly, dropping his cane and nearly losing his balance.

DR. KELLY restrains MR. JACKSON.

MRS. JACKSON *(screams)* Oh my baby, my child! What have you done?

She places both hands on Sonya's face and weeps aloud.

DR. KELLY *(angry)* Nurse! Get them out of here.

NURSE JOHNSON *(yells)* ORDERLY....ORDERLY!
(dashes to the door) Orderly! In here!

NURSE JOHNSON returns and escorts a crying MRS. JACKSON out of the room.

The ORDERLY appears as Mrs. Jackson and the nurse exit. He walks a stunned MR. JACKSON toward the door.

DR. KELLY, bending to examine Sonya, raises his head and speaks to the orderly.

DR. KELLY Take him to my office. I want to talk with him.

He continues to examine Sonya's eyes, pulse, etc.

The lights slowly dim until the stage is completely dark.

End of Scene 2

ACT TWO

Scene 3

RICHARD's voice is heard, **stage right**

RICHARD *(rising voice, anger in it)* Really beautiful, huh, sexy and desirable, right?

The lights come up slowly

INTERROGATION ROOM

(points his finger at the picture of Sonya) Really turns you on, right? Can't understand why I did it? Well, Ill tell you. The goddamned whore is a …

Lights go out suddenly stage right and come up just as suddenly stage center

DR. KELLY'S OFFICE, stage center

MR. JACKSON   MAN!

DR. KELLY   A what?

Lights go out stage center, come up stage right

INTERROGATION ROOM, stage right

BEN   You're crazy.

DETECTIVE #1   No way!

RICHARD   You can't trust them. My father was right. YOU CAN'T TRUST THEM.

SCENE SWITCHES BACK TO
DR. KELLY'S OFFICE, stage center

MR. JACKSON *(head bowed)*   The person you call my daughter, was my son. He had a sex change operation about a year ago.
You brought him…her…into this world. He was your very first delivery – remember?

END OF ACT TWO

ACT THREE

Scene 1, Part One

COURTROOM SCENE

A typical courtroom with table for Defense Attorney and Richard on the left, table for Attorney for the Prosecution on the right. A jury of eight men and women is seated to the right of the prosecution table. The judge's bench is at center stage (rear). An AUDIENCE is present.

Everyone is talking, awaiting the judge, who appears stage left. The trial is in its third day.

BAILIFF (standing stage right)　　Order in the Court. Order in the Court. All rise. This Court is now in session, the Honorable Judge Fairchild presiding.

JUDGE FAIRCHILD enters, takes the bench, raps his gavel, and addresses those assembled in the courtroom.

JUDGE FAIRCHILD　　You may be seated.

(He takes his seat, speaks to Bailiff)　　Bring in the prisoner.

BAILIFF proceeds across to stage left and precedes RICHARD, his attorney, and two guards into the courtroom.

BAILIFF *(suddenly turns to one of the spectators, speaks very loudly and with stern intent)*

Sir!! You must not read the newspaper while this court is in session! Is that clear?

The BAILIFF turns to Richard's table, sees that all are seated and that Richard's handcuffs have been removed. The two GUARDS move off to stage left and stand. The Bailiff then turns to JUDGE FAIRCHILD.

BAILIFF	All is in readiness, Your Honor.
JUDGE FAIRCHILD	Will the attorneys approach the bench?

Both ATTORNEYS approach.

JUDGE FAIRCHILD	Are you both completely ready to proceed?
ATTORNEYS	
JUDGE FAIRCHILD	You have all of your witnesses, exhibits, and evidence?
ATTORNEYS	Yes, Your Honor.
JUDGE FAIRCHILD	Are there any moves for dismissal on any grounds whatsoever at this time?
PROSECUTOR	No, Your Honor.
JUDGE FAIRCHILD	Very well, then, we may proceed. Ms. Prosecutor, call your next witness.

MRS. JACKSON, DEBBIE, and the nurse escort Sonya to a seat. Richard's attorney approaches him and puts a hand on Richard's shoulder, gesturing to him to sit down.

The PROSECUTOR walks back to her table and turns and faces MR. KINGSLEY, who is standing in front of the witness chair.

The BAILIFF approaches MR. KINGSLEY with the Bible in his hand and quietly swears him in.

DEFENSE ATTORNEY

Richard, prepare yourself for the worst. My distinguished colleague has pulled out all the stops, my man, and I do mean all.

RICHARD
(turns and looks at SONYA)

She did it.
Just by walking into this courtroom, she's put me in prison.

DEFENSE ATTORNEY
(looking at MR. KINGSLEY)

And that man ain't going to help you either.

RICHARD

Who is he? I don't even know who he is.

PROSECUTOR

Mr. Kingsley? May we get straight to the point?

(points at Richard)

What, if any, is your relationship to that policeman?

MR. KINGSLEY

I don't know him on a personal level, but he used to work out of the 109th precinct in Queens – plainclothes, narcotics.

He was transferred because I filed a complaint against him earlier this year.

PROSECUTOR	Why did you file a complaint against him? Did he do something to you?
MR. KINGSLEY *(lowers his head, holds back tears)*	No, sir. Not me – but my daughter. He beat my daughter so badly that she lost an eye and she will never walk straight again.
PROSECUTOR	Thank you, Mr. Kingsley, you may step down.
(to the judge)	Your Honor, the Prosecution rests.

She returns to her seat.

JUDGE FAIRCHILD *(to the Defense Attorney)*	Do you wish to cross-examine?
DEFENSE ATTORNEY	No, Your Honor.
JUDGE FAIRCHILD	Are you prepared to present your case?
DEFENSE ATTORNEY	Yes, Your Honor. I have only two witnesses to call, Your Honor; however, I reserve the right to recall any and all previous witnesses and evidence.
JUDGE FAIRCHILD	You may proceed.
DEFENSE ATTORNEY	I call Dr. Roberto Rodriguez
BAILIFF *(approaches audience)*	Dr. Rodriguez, please take the stand.

Dr. Rodriguez goes to the witness stand and is sworn in by the BAILIFF.

MRS. JACKSON Debbie, aren't you going to testify? After all, you know how badly he treated Sonya. Your testimony would put him away for sure.

DEBBIE No, my testimony isn't necessary. He's going to jail, that's for sure.

DEFENSE ATTORNEY Dr. Rodriguez, would you explain your connection with this case?

DR. RODRIGUEZ I am the surgeon who performed the sex reassignment surgery on Charles Sonny Jackson, now legally and in every other way a true woman, now named Sonya.

I performed her surgery just over a year ago, and she has been one of my best post-ops to date. That is, she has had no medical problems at all.

RICHARD hangs his head

DEFENSE ATTORNEY Have you seen Sonya lately?

DR. RODRIGUEZ Yes, I was called in by Dr. Kelly, for consultation and also to observe an examination of Sonya, after she was admitted to the hospital with various and multiple injuries.

DEFENSE ATTORNEY In your expert opinion, did Sonya Jackson receive any internal injuries that would jeopardize her new status as a woman?

DR. RODRIGUEZ Oh... No. All of her injuries were external, except for the head injury. She may suffer...ah...

DEFENSE ATTORNEY
(interrupts)

Please, Doctor, just answer yes or no from this point on. Did Sonya receive any internal injuries that would jeopardize her present status as a full-fledged woman?

DR. RODRIGUEZ No.

DEFENSE ATTORNEY When Dr. Kelly testified, he stated that he examined Sonya from head to foot, internally and externally. And he was totally surprised to learn that Sonya was once a man.

In your expert opinion, is this normal? That is to say, if a doctor with twenty years' experience and knowledge couldn't tell that Sonya was once a man, how could an ordinary layman like Richard know?

DR. RODRIGUEZ Well, in most cases a layman would not know. Once these individuals have reached the stage where they are acceptable for sex reassignment surgery, they are ninety percent woman in mind and body.
In my expert opinion, there is no way a layman or most doctors could tell. Not without a detailed internal examination using the most modern equipment available.

DEFENSE ATTORNEY Even during intercourse?

DR. RODRIGUEZ Yes, sir, even during intercourse. If the surgery is performed properly and the latest method is used, there is no difference.

(Everyone reacts – gasps, whispers, laughs.)

DEFENSE ATTORNEY How many such operations have you performed, Doctor?

DR. RODRIGUEZ To date, one hundred seventy-six.

(Audience reaction)

DEFENSE ATTORNEY All were surgically successful?

DR. RODRIGUEZ Yes, but a few had mental lapses because they were disappointed that they still hadn't found happiness. This operation isn't for everyone, only a chosen few.

DEFENSE ATTORNEY Only a chosen few!! Of those so-called chosen few, are there any present in this courtroom today, other than Sonya?

DR. RODRIGUEZ
(hesitates, looks around) Yes, I see three. Of course, I will not identify them, because for most of them their past lives are something they don't want revealed. Especially if they've found happiness after living most of their lives in the body of a male, when they know in their hearts and minds that they are really female – or vice versa.

DEFENSE ATTORNEY You mean!

DR. RODRIGUEZ Yes, there are also women who have sex reassignment surgery and become full-fledged males.

PROSECUTOR Objection, Your Honor. This testimony is wholly irrelevant to this case. Defense is trying to play on the sympathy of this jury by clouding the facts of this case with a lot of medical mumbo-jumbo.

JUDGE FAIRCHILD Sustained.

(to the stenographer) Strike the last statement made by the doctor. All other statements are pertinent and shall remain.

(to the DEFENSE ATTORNEY) However, I will direct the defense attorney to only bring forth facts that are pertinent to these proceedings. Be advised that you must proceed with caution.

DEFENSE ATTORNEY
(lowers his head) Yes, Your Honor.

(turns to DR. RODRIGUEZ) Thank you, Doctor. Your testimony has been most enlightening.

(looks at Prosecutor) Cross-examine?

PROSECUTOR I have no questions at this time.

JUDGE FAIRCHILD You may step down, Doctor.

(to the Defense Attorney) Call your next witness.

Dr. Rodriguez returns to his seat in the audience.

DEFENSE ATTORNEY   May it please the Court. I must inform all present that the next witness I call may be considered hostile at worst, and reluctant at best. Nevertheless, in the interest of my client's freedom, I must call upon this person.

DEFENSE ATTORNEY approaches the BAILIFF and whispers in his ear. A hush comes over the courtroom.

BAILIFF *(walks toward audience)*   I call Robert Dancy to the stand.

No one stands. The spectators begin to look at each other, murmuring among themselves.

BAILIFF *(louder)*   I call Robert Dancy -----Mr. Robert Dancy.

DEFENSE ATTORNEY *(to judge)*   Your Honor, would you please direct Mr. Robert Dancy to take the stand.

JUDGE FAIRCHILD   Which individual is it?

DEFENSE ATTORNEY walks toward the JUDGE – and as he does, DEBBIE stands quickly, and very proudly and ceremoniously takes the witness stand. The audience is in an uproar. The JUDGE calls for order. Even MRS. JACKSON shows disbelief.

BAILIFF   Do you solemnly swear to tell the truth, the whole truth, and nothing but the truth, so help you God?

DEBBIE   I do.

BAILIFF   State your name.

DEBBIE Robert Charles Dancy

BAILIFF Be seated.

DEFENSE ATTORNEY Mr. Dancy, I described you as a hostile witness. Would you be good enough to explain to this court why?

DEBBIE Isn't it obvious? Here I sit, a woman in every way, but because I ran out of money after I had my operation, I couldn't get my name legally changed to Deborah Dancy.

That's why I didn't want to testify. I knew that I would be called by my legal name, and all those people who have known me for the past two years as Debbie will now know my real name and laugh behind my back. And the real mean ones, those who don't care about a person's feelings, will laugh in my face.

DEFENSE ATTORNEY I'm sorry, ... Debbie. But I have no choice, especially since you were the first person on the scene after the tragic incident of which my client is accused.

DEBBIE *(irate)* Accused. Accused! He's guilty just as sure as my name is Deb...... Well, he's guilty.

DEFENSE ATTORNEY Debbie, I want you to think and think hard.

Now tell me, did you actually see my client in that apartment when you entered and found your friend so brutally beaten?

Did you actually see Richard's face….or just the shape of a man going through the window, that looked like Richard?

DEBBIE starts to speak, then drops her head; hesitates, looks at SONYA, then looks at the attorney.

DEBBIE I was so upset from hearing the uproar.

DEFENSE ATTORNEY Just answer the question, please.

DEBBIE *(looks at SONYA, speaks softly)* All I saw was the figure of a man.

DEFENSE ATTORNEY Thank you.

DEBBIE *(stands, points at RICHARD)* But it was you. I know it was you!

JUDGE FAIRCHILD Young lady. You are out of order. Take your seat.

(audience starts to get restless) Order in the court. Order in the court! Once again, I must instruct the jury to disregard the last statement of a witness.

But this time, I do so with a warning that this behavior will no longer be tolerated in my courtroom. The next time there is an outburst of this sort, I will clear the courtroom and declare a mistrial. Is that understood?

(He adjusts his robe, sticks out his chest, raps the gavel, and turns to the Defense Attorney)

You may proceed.

(He takes his seat.)

DEFENSE ATTORNEY   Just for the record, Your Honor, could we hear the answer that the witness gave just before the outburst?

STENOGRAPHER   The witness stated that all she saw was the figure of a man.

DEFENSE ATTORNEY   Thank you. I have no further questions for this witness at this time.

(to Prosecutor)   Cross-examine?

PROSECUTOR   Now, Miss Dancy, why are you so certain that the man you saw going out of the window in Sonya's apartment was the defendant?

DEFENSE ATTORNEY   Objection. That part of her testimony was stricken.

PROSECUTOR   I'll rephrase the question. While Sonya and Richard were seeing each other (dating), how many times did you actually see Richard?

DEBBIE   Oh, eight or ten, easily.

PROSECUTOR   Do you recall the very first time that you saw him?

DEBBIE   Oh, yes, I'll never forget that night.

PROSECUTOR   Would you explain to this court what you mean by that statement?

DEBBIE   Sure will. I was managing a night club. I got Sonya a job there as a dancer.

Well, she had just gone on stage, when all of a sudden, out of nowhere, the cops pulled a drug raid.
Some were in uniform and some not. They were everywhere. We knew that there was no sense running. So, we all relaxed and prepared ourselves to be arrested.

All but Sonya. You see, this was her first raid. She panicked and started to run. She ran right into Richard. He grabbed her, threw her to the floor and was about to pistol-whip her, then he just stopped and stared at her.

Now, Renee, Mr. Kingsley's daughter, thought she could keep Sonya from getting a beating by helping her to her feet, but when she touched Sonya, Richard became irate.

He hit Renee right in the face with his gun. Then, when she fell to the floor, he kicked her like she was no more than a football.

He kicked her and kicked her again and again and again. I wanted to help her but one of the uniformed cops stopped me. I yelled at him, "You stop him. He's killing her!"

The uniformed cop just stood there. Finally, it was over when one of the detectives yelled out, "Here comes the Captain." Richard just stood over Renee, who didn't know whether to hold her face or her leg. Then he reached down and grabbed Sonya. I thought he was going to beat her, too. But instead, he helped her up and led her right past some of his fellow barbarians and let her leave. I heard him tell her to go home and he would see her later. The rest of us went to jail.

PROSECUTOR So after that initial time you saw this man some eight or ten times more over a period of how long?

DEBBIE About three and a half months…

PROSECUTOR *(turns to the jury)* Ladies and gentlemen, I submit to you that this young lady did recognize the defendant as the man leaving Sonya's apartment by the window, on the night that he committed the brutal and heinous act upon my client, Sonya Jackson. There is absolutely no doubt in my mind, and I'm sure that you feel the same way.

DEFENSE ATTORNEY Objection.

PROSECUTOR I withdraw my last statement. You may step down, Ms. Dancy.

DEBBIE stands, proceeds toward the audience. She stops, reaches out to SONYA, embraces her.

ACT THREE

Scene 1, Part Two

When the lights rise again, court is already in session and DR. SUSSMAN is on the stand.

All others are in place.

DEFENSE ATTORNEY   Dr. Sussman, you are the psychiatrist who counseled Sonya Jackson both before and after she received her sex change operation. Are you not?

DR. SUSSMAN   I am.

DEFENSE ATTORNEY   And you have counseled Miss Jackson since she last entered the hospital?

DR. SUSSMAN   I have.

DEFENSE ATTORNEY   What, if anything, can you tell this court about Sonya's mental state as it is now, compared to what it was, oh say a year ago?

DR. SUSSMAN — Well, a year ago, Sonya's mental state was very shaky. She had just received her operation, and naturally she was very apprehensive about the outcome. At the same time, she was really happy that she had gone through the operation.

DEFENSE ATTORNEY — Please, Doctor, just tell us what her mental state was a year ago and what her mental state is now.

DR. SUSSMAN — She was unstable then and she was unstable the last time I spoke to her last week.

DEFENSE ATTORNEY — Is this instability permanent?

DR. SUSSMAN — Oh no, I'm certain she will regain her confidence and self-esteem in a very short time.

DEFENSE ATTORNEY — By a short time, do you mean today, tomorrow, next month, next year? Can you be specific?

DR. SUSSMAN — No, you know I can't be specific. It all depends on how soon she can put this trauma behind her.

DEFENSE ATTORNEY — Now Doctor, please. To my next question, please answer with a simple yes or no.

In your professional opinion, in Sonya's present state of mind, is she competent to take the witness stand?

PROSECUTOR Objection. Your Honor, counsel is asking the witness to make a conclusion.

JUDGE FAIRCHILD Overruled. What is your answer, Doctor?

DR. SUSSMAN No.

JUDGE FAIRCHILD Very simply, if she were to testify, and he…

(points to the Defense Attorney) were to examine her, her mental state could only deteriorate under the strain.

DEFENSE ATTORNEY
(leans toward Richard and whispers) Now we've got a good chance.

(turns to Prosecutor) Your witness.

PROSECUTOR Dr. Sussman. How long have you known Sonya?

DR. SUSSMAN Just shy of six years.

PROSECUTOR So you knew her some five years before she had her surgery.

DR. SUSSMAN Yes.

PROSECUTOR Is it normal for psychiatrists to know their patients that far in advance of their receiving sex reassignment surgery?

DR. SUSSMAN Yes, I have some patients that I counsel up to ten years in advance of surgery. Some never go through with the surgery. Some never go through with the surgery, even after years of counseling.

PROSECUTOR	Is ten years a normal waiting period?
DR. SUSSMAN	No, it isn't. Sonya's waiting period is more than the norm.
PROSECUTOR	Why did you say that Sonya shouldn't testify? Is it because you fear for her future mental state?
DR. SUSSMAN	Definitely. Her testimony could win the case, but she would lose something more important.
DEFENSE ATTORNEY	Objection.
JUDGE FAIRCHILD	Sustained. The jury is instructed to disregard the doctor's last remark. Ms. Prosecutor, what is the objective of this line of questioning? What are you leading to?
PROSECUTOR	Your Honor, my client has expressed a desire to testify. The doctor's testimony has jeopardized the validity of anything that my client is in fact competent to testify to.
JUDGE FAIRCHILD	Proceed!!
PROSECUTOR	If it please the court, I have a letter that my client wrote, and I would like to place it into evidence at this time.

PROSECUTOR passes the letter to the BAILIFF, who takes the letter to the STENOGRAPHER.
She stamps it, gives it back to the BAILIFF, who takes it to the JUDGE. He looks at it, nods his approval, and gives it back to the BAILIFF, who gives it back to the PROSECUTOR.

PROSECUTOR
(approaches Dr. Sussman, hands him the letter) Do you recognize this letter?

DR. SUSSMAN
(looks at the letter for a moment Yes, I do. It's a letter that was written by Sonya. I had it published in a medical journal because I thought it was that good.

PROSECUTOR Would you be kind enough to read this letter to the court, please.

DR. SUSSMAN Of course.
(He reads the letter)

On September 5th, 1984, I finally became a full-fledged woman, and this is my story.

At the age of twelve, I found myself in church on my knees at the altar. But I wasn't praying to God for forgiveness.

I was actually pleading with God to show me the way that I could align my physical body to my mind, my very self, which was female. I knew on that day that I wanted to be a female more than anything, and why not? I've always felt more like a female than a male, even when I was very young—four or five.

At first, at about four years of age, I just felt different, as though I didn't belong. I was always lonely because I desired to play with girls, but they didn't want to play with me, and I was never accepted by the boys in my age group. Consequently, I stayed in the house and learned whatever I could from my mother.

I used to ask my mother many questions about many topics and she, not being the most worldly of mothers, would tell me to ask my father for the answers.

That, I hesitated to do, because my father worked two jobs and when he came home, he usually went directly to bed. On the few occasions that I did get to talk to him, he always seemed to reject me or at least put me off, by telling me to read a book to obtain the information I wanted.

I felt that my father's actions were demoralizing to me because I was sure that he knew that in every way but biologically, I was a female. Even so, I still yearned for his affection and his approval of me as I was, but that was something I never received. I have a vague memory of him harshly scolding me, for playing with a male doll—a toy—that was dressed in an Army uniform. It was then that I reached the point of no return. It was then that his approval no longer mattered to me.

It was then that I began to accept, in small steps, who I was and who I was going to be.

As I grew older and became even more aware of my sexuality, I began to hate my physical body. I suffered from moments of depression and even thought about committing suicide on several occasions.

Not possessing enough courage to take that final step, I did what I considered to be the next best thing—self- mutilation—with the hope that this would lead to my ultimate goal, surgical removal of my penis. But to my dismay, I was merely treated at a local hospital and released, on three different occasions.

As time passed, I found myself always making resentful comments about medical doctors who (I felt) knew what I wanted and needed, but they would not give to me.

One day, I decided to stop cursing the darkness and seek some real help. I paid a visit to a psychiatrist. I convinced him that I knew what I wanted but didn't know how to go about getting it.

After six months of consultation, the psychiatrist told me that he was truly convinced that I should be a female and that he would help me to achieve that goal with all of the resources that he had.

On my next visit, he asked if I had ever heard of Christine Jorgensen. I answered no. He commenced to tell me her story. He told me her entire story and I was absolutely flabbergasted.

She was the first true Transsexual.

Then he popped the question --- "Would you like to go through the sex change operation?" I quickly answered, "Yes, yes, Oh God, yes!" I jumped up and gave a joyous shout of relief, then ran over and embraced him. "When may I start? – when can I become a woman in body as well as mind?" He said, "Calm down, it's a very slow and involved process."

He began to explain.

First of all, there's an interview with a Hospital Board of Directors, which must be arranged before anything else can take place. He made the arrangements.

Would you believe that when I went for the interview, the staff doctors actually tried to test my intelligence and my awareness of what I've wanted for a lifetime?

They were soon convinced that I knew where my head was. Then we got down to cases. "This is what will take place.

"First of all, your name goes on a four-year waiting list for the operation. You'll be subjected to psychiatric testing continuously for seven to ten days, 24 hours a day, that's step #2. Then, as you approach step #3, in your third year, you must do the following.

"You must give us your entire personal history from your first breath to this very moment. Physical, neurological, and routine lab studies will be conducted.

"Photos will be taken of you dressed as both a male and a female and also in the nude. You'll be recorded on videotape stating your problems, and also the reason you desire sex reassignment surgery.

"All of this information will be presented before the Board in six months' time, after you have completed step #3, and they, and only they, will make a recommendation to go forward, if they feel you can cope, or to cease and desist, before moving on to step #4."

Six months later, I had saved up $6,000 and was waiting to hear from the Board. The chief surgeon called and casually, oh so casually, informed me that we were now ready to proceed with step #4. I was so overjoyed that I dropped the phone! By the time I picked it up again, he was already mapping out step #4.

I had to enter the hospital for a short time, for retesting of the urine, and so on. I was to receive my first estrogen shot, then be released under the care of my own doctor for another six months while the shots continued.

Those estrogen shots were really something. They made my skin smoother. I shaved less and less. My voice became more feminine and my entire body began to take on a more feminine appearance.

I was advised to retain an attorney for legal counseling on the operative permit and change of name (legally). I was told that now I had to dress completely feminine for the duration of phase two. Also, during this time, I was to make a final decision by and for myself–should I or shouldn't I?

Needless to say, my mind was already made up and I was anxiously waiting for step #4 to begin.

I did come up with one request, however: I wanted videotape and still photographs of the actual procedure as it was taking place. I wanted to be the first person to witness his or her own rebirth.

I nearly had a heart attack when the chief surgeon informed me that everything was A-O-K and asked jokingly, "Why are you taking so long to get admitted for surgery?"

The next day, I was there with bells on. The chief surgeon explained that it would be done in one step, which would take about two hours.

After the operation was completed, I remained asleep for nearly twelve hours. When I awakened, it took some time before I realized where I was and what I was there for. A nurse walked past, and I called out to her.

She turned and said, "Yes, Miss?" I didn't hear another word after that, because then, FOR THE FIRST TIME IN MY LIFE, I realized that I was finally A WOMAN. I became so excited that I had to be sedated to keep from hurting myself in my joy and ecstasy. September 5th,1984—the day that I was RE-BORN.

The next time I awakened, my psychiatrist was at my bedside. He said to me, "You're the largest newborn person I've ever seen." Then he asked, "How do you feel, Sonya?"

All I could do was smile. Then he said, "You're all right, you're just fine, and in a week or so, you'll be going home."

PROSECUTOR	Thank you, Doctor. I can see why you had the letter published. It is rather touching.
JUDGE FAIRCHILD	Ms. Prosecutor, this court has been very patient, but my endurance is waning. Please make your point.
PROSECUTOR	Yes, Your Honor. Now, Doctor, how many days after her operation, would you say, did Sonya write this letter?
DR. SUSSMAN	She told me, three days.
PROSECUTOR	And isn't that type of operation (sex reassignment surgery) an extremely traumatic experience?
DR. SUSSMAN	Yes, of course.

PROSECUTOR	And in your professional opinion, was your patient rational when she wrote this letter?
DR. SUSSMAN	Yes, she was.
PROSECUTOR	Then, I put it to you, Doctor, that if Sonya Jackson was competent after going through the ordeal of a life-changing, body-changing, mind-changing experience such as that, and could still be rational after only three days….. How could you say that she was not mentally stable enough, after going through the horrific beating that she took at the hands of that man *(points at RICHARD)*, when it is now three weeks later. Not just three days, but three whole weeks.
DR. SUSSMAN	She was, ah….
PROSECUTOR	I have no further questions.
DR. SUSSMAN	But, I want….
PROSECUTOR	You may step down, Doctor.
(turns to JUDGE FAIRCHILD)	I wish to call Miss Sonya Jackson.
JUDGE FAIRCHILD	Ms. Prosecutor, must this court remind you that the defense has not relinquished the floor?
(looks at DEFENSE ATTORNEY)	Cross-examination, sir?
DEFENSE ATTORNEY	No, Your Honor. I call Miss Sonya Jackson.

(whispers to RICHARD)   I have to break her down.

BAILIFF moves forward, goes over and assists a slowly moving SONYA, who keeps staring at RICHARD.

BAILIFF   Do you swear….

SONYA   I swear, I swear.

BAILIFF looks at the JUDGE, who gestures OK

DEFENSE ATTORNEY *(sarcastically)*   Sonya Jackson…ARE YOU A MAN OR A WOMAN?

PROSECUTOR   Objection, Your Honor. Defense is badgering the witness.

SONYA *(surprised)*   I'm a woman.

DEFENSE ATTORNEY   Are you frigid?

SONYA   No, but I've only had sex once since my…

DEFENSE ATTORNEY   Are you trying to get this esteemed jury to believe that Richard is the only man you ever slept with?

SONYA   Yes.

DEFENSE ATTORNEY   Did my client beat you?

SONYA   Yes, he did!

DEFENSE ATTORNEY   Do you know why?

SONYA   No, we made love and it was totally beautiful. I couldn't believe that things went as well as they did.

DEFENSE ATTORNEY   What happened then?

SONYA We talked for a while, then he turned on the radio (a talk show). We talked a little more. Made love again. Then I fell asleep.

The next thing I knew, Richard was hitting me. He hit me all over. Everywhere, my head, my body, my legs…my back.

(very emotional) Then, he pushed me onto the floor and kicked me in my face and back. He hit me in the back of my head with the lamp from my night table. It shattered.

Then he pulled me back on the bed and beat me some more. All the time he kept saying "YOU CAN'T TRUST THEM, YOU CAN'T TRUST THEM!

I tried to get away, but I couldn't move. I tried to call for help, and he choked me.

That's all I remember.

DEFENSE ATTORNEY How long did you and Richard date?

SONYA Nearly four months.

DEFENSE ATTORNEY And during that period of time, did he ever lay a hand on you in anger?

SONYA No.

DEFENSE ATTORNEY And did you tell your friends that he was really good to you?

SONYA Yes, I did, but….

DEFENSE ATTORNEY And when you first met him at the night club, didn't he allow you to escape without punishment of any kind?

PROSECUTOR Objection. Defense is leading the witness.

JUDGE FAIRCHILD Sustained. Defense's tactics are not illegal; however, this court would like to hear the witness say something more than yes or no.

DEFENSE ATTORNEY Now, Sonya, in your own words, would you tell this court if Richard was ever cruel to you.

SONYA Before that night, he never put his hands on me in anger.

DEFENSE ATTORNEY Please tell this court what else he did for you.

SONYA Well, he got my best friend Debbie out of jail. Bought me flowers and candy and took me out every once in a while.

DEFENSE ATTORNEY Did he ever try to force himself on you?

SONYA No, he never forced himself on me.

DEFENSE ATTORNEY   Now Sonya, you stated before that you were a full-fledged woman, and I feel that you are a beautiful woman and I'm sure that Richard felt the same way.

My question to you is, how did you manage to keep him at arm's length for nearly four months?

What did you tell him, so he wouldn't, well, you know?

SONYA *(drops her head) (raises her head and looks straight at the ATTORNEY)*   Yes, I know.

I lied to him. I told him I was sick, and I told him I didn't feel like it. I told him I had women's problems; I told him anything I could think of because I wanted to wait one full year before attempting intercourse.

DEFENSE ATTORNEY   One full year from what?

SONYA   My operation. My Rebirth.

DEFENSE ATTORNEY   What about your little brother who died?

SONYA   No, in a way that wasn't a lie. I was referring to the fact that my male being was dead and gone, and my new female form was alive and well.

DEFENSE ATTORNEY   Well, you may not call that a lie, but I do. In fact, you have, with your very own testimony, proven beyond a shadow of a doubt that even though my client treated you with the utmost respect, all you did was lie to him and deceive him.

PROSECUTOR   Objection. The question here is if the defendant brutally attacked my client.

JUDGE FAIRCHILD   Overruled.

(addresses the PROSECUTOR)   Do you wish to cross-examine?

PROSECUTOR *approaches the witness stand.*

SONYA   May I have some water, please?

BAILIFF approaches SONYA, pours a glass of water, and passes it to her. SONYA seems to choke on the water and begins to cough. She coughs louder and longer. Her NURSE goes to her side, as she continues to cough.

NURSE *(to JUDGE FAIRCHILD)*   May I take her to the first aid room?

JUDGE FAIRCHILD   Very well. Court will recess for twenty minutes.

BAILIFF   All rise. *(pauses)* Twenty minutes, folks. Twenty minutes.

The JUDGE and JURY leave.

AUDIENCE remains seated. A few may go out and return quickly.

ATTORNEYS and clients remain at their tables.

The NURSE and DEBBIE escort SONYA, weak and still coughing, to the first aid room. MRS. JACKSON follows.

DEFENSE ATTORNEY stands and slaps RICHARD on the back.

DEFENSE ATTORNEY Don't worry. Things are looking good, real good.

RICHARD Well, I'm glad you feel confident, because I sure don't. If I were on that jury watching that girl…*(angrily)*…that guy…cry, and seeing how bad he/she looks, I'd be inclined to lean in her direction.

DEFENSE ATTORNEY Thanks for the vote of confidence in me. I've done all I can do to make you look like a saint. I brought out all of your good points. And the best part about it is, all your good points came from the mouth of your victim.

RICHARD *(irate0* See! See!! Even you call her my victim. Even after I told you why I did it. Put yourself in my position. Wouldn't you have done the same thing?

DEFENSE ATTORNEY OK, Richard. It sounds to me like you want to testify in your own behalf, even though I feel that it would be a big mistake.

RICHARD I feel that if the jury knew the reason, then they could understand my actions.

DEFENSE ATTORNEY	You're wrong, Richard. They've been instructed in the law of this case by Judge Fairchild. They'll be looking only at whether you did it or not. That comes first. Then they look for the reason. And frankly, your reason isn't strong enough.
RICHARD	Well, it's my life on the line. And I believe I should testify.
DEFENSE ATTORNEY	You're sure? Absolutely sure?
RICHARD *(hesitates)*	Yes, I'm sure.
DEFENSE ATTORNEY	OK, Richard, I'll put you on the stand as soon as Sonya finishes testifying. But I will only ask you questions that lead up the incident, then I want you to say why you did it, but you must promise me that you won't linger. Just come right out with it. Then be prepared to be cross-examined. And please, Richard, answer only the questions that you're asked. Don't elaborate on anything.

Action pauses, as everyone sits quietly, waiting for the JUDGE and JURY to return

BAILIFF re-enters	All rise. This court is now in session.

BAILIFF returns to stage right as JUDGE FAIRCHILD enters and sits.

JUDGE FAIRCHILD	I have been informed by the nurse that Sonya cannot resume the stand at this time. Perhaps she can before these proceedings have come to an end today.

Therefore, in the interest of time and justice, I ask if both attorneys if they would be in agreement and allow this case to proceed. If there is any dissension, then we will dismiss for the day and reconvene tomorrow at ten a.m.

Both attorneys move to center stage. They confer, then face the judge.

DEFENSE ATTORNEY	We would like to continue, Your Honor.

JUDGE FAIRCHILD	Very well.

Both attorneys take their positions.

DEFENSE ATTORNEY	I call Richard Santiago Miller

Richard stands and quickly walks to the witness stand.

BAILIFF	Do you solemnly swear to tell the truth, the whole truth, and nothing but the truth, so help you God?

RICHARD	I do.

BAILIFF	Be seated.

DEFENSE ATTORNEY	Richard, do you deny that you are the man accused of hitting Sonya Jackson?

RICHARD	I have been so accused, yes sir.

(DEFENSE ATTORNEY kind of sneers at Richard because of his long answer.)

DEFENSE ATTORNEY	On the night in question, did you and Sonya engage in normal sexual activity?

RICHARD	Yes, we did. (*turns to the Judge*) Your Honor, I would like to speak freely, say what's on my mind, and get this thing over with. May I, sir?
DEFENSE ATTORNEY	I object, Your Honor. My client is….
JUDGE FAIRCHILD	If the defendant wishes to do so, he may. However, I have a question that I would like to ask.
(*clears his throat*)	Am I to understand that during the sexual act, there was no difference, none at all?

DEFENSE ATTORNEY throws his hands up and takes his seat, looking totally disgusted. He jumps to his feet.

DEFENSE ATTORNEY	Don't answer that question, Richard.

RICHARD looks around for SONYA. Not seeing her in the courtroom, he answers the question.

The DEFENSE ATTORNEY squirms in his chair as Richard elaborates.

RICHARD	Sonya and I dated for nearly four months. On the night in question, we were out on the town having a good time. When we got to her apartment door, I dumped her pocketbook in the hallway, so we could find the key to her apartment. While I was looking for her key, Sonya picked up an appointment card from a doctor. I took it from her and asked if she was sick. She said, "NO! It's just for a checkup."

I didn't think anything of it at the time. Then later, after we made love a second time, Sonya fell asleep. I lay there listening to the talk show that was on the radio. To my surprise, the doctor whose name was on the card was on the radio. The same doctor who testified in this courtroom earlier today, Dr. Rodriguez.

He said that he had performed 143 sex change operations up to that time. He also said that he recommended to all of his patients that they be examined every three months after surgery, and he cautioned his patients to wait at least one year before attempting intercourse, if they wanted the best results.

I lay there a while, then I put two and two together and because I am a good cop, I knew that I was in bed with a MAN.

I couldn't control myself. I tried, believe me, I tried. I shook her. She wouldn't wake up. I shook her again. And she just wouldn't respond.

I don't remember exactly what happened after that, until I decided to get the hell out of that place as quickly as I could.

That's when she woke up and tried to make me stay. That's when I lost it completely, and all I could think of was my father beating on my mother and making me hit her also.

That's the scene that I think of every time I get angry. And to answer your question, Your Honor, there was no difference. The sex was the bomb!

As the audience begins reacting to Richard's testimony, there's a stir in the back of the courtroom, and a middle-aged man and woman—JERRY and LOLITA--enter, walk to the front of the courtroom and start looking for seats in the front row. The BAILIFF quickly approaches them and motions for them to find seats in the back of the room.

BAILIFF   Sir, Madam! This section of seats is reserved. Please find places in the back row.

JERRY *(loudly)*   We are RICHARD Miller's parents, here to support our son.

Everyone in the room stirs, stares at the newcomers, begins to murmur.

BAILIFF   Order in the court!

BAILIFF looks inquiringly at JUDGE FAIRCHILD, who nods OK, lifts his hands and shrugs.
The BAILIFF begins to move people from two seats at the end of the front row. There's confusion, annoyance in the AUDIENCE. People stand up to get a better view of what is going on at the front of the courtroom.

JUDGE FAIRCHILD   Order in the court! Order in the court!

LOLITA and JERRY sit, then LOLITA suddenly grabs JERRY's arm, points at JUDGE FAIRCHILD, leans over and speaks in JERRY's ear. She gets up, tries to squeeze past Jerry to get to the aisle.

JERRY stands up, takes a swing at his wife as she gets into the aisle, then starts toward JUDGE FAIRCHILD, intent on doing serious damage.

JERRY (yelling)   It was you, it was YOU in my apartment 21 years ago!

JUDGE FAIRCHILD   LOLITA?!

The BAILIFF stops JERRY before he reaches the rail around the bench, motions for GUARDS to come restrain him and escort him from the courtroom.

LOLITA disappears.

Pandemonium erupts in the courtroom.

RICHARD – still in the witness stand – sits stunned, stares as JERRY is taken out of the courtroom, turns to see if LOLITA is still there. He looks back at the judge, ready to resume his testimony.

Just then, SONYA appears stage right.

She's alone. She approaches the jury box, walking very unsteadily without her cane. She seems unaware of the dramatic events going on.

JUDGE FAIRCHILD sits back down and simply watches SONYA.

The AUDIENCE, exhausted, is stunned into silence, then the courtroom begins to buzz again.

JUDGE FAIRCHILD (shaken, but (pulls himself together, raps his gavel)   Order, order in the court! ORDER IN THE COURT!

SONYA (to the JUDGE and JURY)   I know I'm out of order, but I had to finish my testimony.

(She leans against the jury box and points to RICHARD)

> That man beat me. That man nearly killed me, and for that, I hate him.

RICHARD *(points back at SONYA)* I hate you too!

SONYA *(to the JURY)*

> But even so, you can't find him guilty. Why?
>
> Because I never told him. I never told him that I had been a woman trapped in a man's body.
>
> I tried. I tried many times, but I never told him.

RICHARD *(stands, staring at SONYA, pointing a finger at her)*

> SEE! SEE!! That's why she got beat up. She never told me that she was once a man. If she had, I would never have taken her out or anything. She should've told me; she should have told me!
>
> You can't trust them! You can't trust them!

SONYA suddenly slumps to the floor. Her nurse and mother rush to her side. Chaos erupts in the courtroom.

PROSECUTOR
(stands, yells at Judge)

Mistrial! You should declare a mistrial!

The BAILIFF approaches JUDGE FAIRCHILD to protect him, as the AUDIENCE members get out of control.
DEBBIE rushes toward RICHARD with bad intentions, but is restrained by Richard's two GUARDS.

JUDGE FAIRCHILD
(pounding his gavel)

Order! Order!!!
Order in my courtroom or I'll have this courtroom cleared!

(glares at PROSECUTOR)

Ms. Prosecutor, this is my court, and I'll conduct it as I see fit. Now, please be seated.

(He huffs)

Mistrial, indeed!

PROSECUTOR sits.

RICHARD *is removed from the witness stand by his two* GUARDS. SONYA *is taken away by her* NURSE *and* MRS. JACKSON.

JUDGE FAIRCHILD *regains composure, settles in his seat, and resumes as if nothing unusual had happened.*

JUDGE FAIRCHILD

At this time, I call for closing arguments.

DEFENSE ATTORNEY *(stands)*

I pass, Your Honor.

PROSECUTOR *(stands)*
(throws up her arms in disgust)

I also pass, Your Honor.
What's the use?!

The JUDGE *stares at the* PROSECUTOR. *Then he stares at the* DEFENSE ATTORNEY.

JUDGE FAIRCHILD *(angrily)*

Be seated.

(to the jury, soberly, respectfully))

Ladies and gentlemen of the jury, you are about to be charged. You've been given the law concerning this case, and you are aware that your only responsibility is to establish, beyond a reasonable doubt, the guilt or innocence of the defendant.

	It will be up to this court to pass the sentence, if any is forthcoming. Take your time and come back with a just verdict.
BAILIFF	Would the jury please rise?

JURORS rise; BAILIFF goes to open the swinging door to the jury box. The JURY FOREMAN speaks softly to the BAILIFF, and the two men move offstage briefly. The other jurors remain standing.

No one else moves.

DEFENSE ATTORNEY *(to RICHARD)*	Well, Richard, I hope it turns out in your favor.
RICHARD	After all that, what verdict can I expect? What possible kind of sentence can I expect to receive from this judge, of all people?!

BAILIFF and JURY FOREMAN re-enter. FOREMAN resumes his seat in the jury box. All jurors sit.

BAILIFF walks to the Judge's bench and whispers in JUDGE FAIRCHILD's ear. He has a sheet of paper in his hand.

BAILIFF steps down to center stage

BAILIFF	Order in the court. Order in the court!

He moves to stage left and stands, then addresses JUDGE FAIRCHILD formally.

BAILIFF	Your Honor, the jury has made a decision.

JUDGE FAIRCHILD
(to BAILIFF)

Already?! Please pass up the verdict.

BAILIFF takes the sheet of paper to the STENOGRAPHER, who stamps it, records it, returns it to the BAILIFF, who takes it to the JUDGE.

JUDGE FAIRCHILD

Ladies and gentlemen. It seems that the jury has made up its mind and is ready to render its decision. Mr. Foreman. What is your verdict?

JURY FOREMAN *(stands)*

We the jury find the defendant guilty as charged on all counts.

RICHARD jumps to his feet. The two GUARDS place their hands on RICHARD's shoulders. He sits and extends his arms to his guards to be cuffed. The audience gets noisy.

JUDGE FAIRCHILD *(to the jury)*

Thank you, ladies and gentlemen. You've not only done an honorable job in rendering your services as jurors, but in addition, you have served your community well. You now stand discharged as jurors in this case, and you have my personal thanks for a job well done. You are now dismissed.

JURY exits, led by BAILIFF, who returns to his position at stage left.

JUDGE FAIRCHILD *(to the audience)*

Like the jury, I have had to weigh the facts in this case and I, too, have reached a decision which I feel is fair and just for this defendant.

BAILIFF

Would the defendant please rise.

RICHARD stands, cuffed, dejected, apprehensive, head hanging low. He moves to center stage.

JUDGE FAIRCHILD   It is the opinion of this court that the defendant is in need of psychiatric testing.

RICHARD stands straight and stares at the judge.

I therefore recommend that Richard Santiago Miller be admitted to the minimum-security Psychological Hospital in midtown Manhattan for observation and testing.

I also recommend that he remain suspended from his job for the duration of his stay in that institution and that if he does return to his employment, he be placed on office work status only.

This court stands adjourned.

JUDGE FAIRCHILD raps his gavel, stands, raps his gavel again.

Stage slowly goes dark

END OF COURTROOM SCENE

End of ACT THREE, Scene 1

ACT THREE

Scene 2

Sonya's apartment

SONYA is getting dressed, humming a tune – "HEY WORLD." She zips up her dress, walks over to a full-length mirror. Admires herself.

There's a knock on her door.

DEBBIE	(*almost in song*) It's me, your neighbor!
SONYA	Come on in – it's not locked.
DEBBIE	Oh Sonya, you look so beautiful!
SONYA	WHO, ME?

She turns, looks in the mirror, runs her hands down the sides of her dress.

She likes what she sees!	YES, ME!
DEBBIE	Going out?

SONYA Yeah, I think I'll go uptown and see my mother *(smile fades)*—that's if she's alone.

She takes her coat from the couch. DEBBIE precedes her out of the door.

BACK PROJECTION

***SONYA** is seen outside her apartment building, hailing a cab. She gets into the cab, gives instructions to the driver, rides through streets to her parents' apartment house, pays driver, gets out of the cab, walks to the door, rings bell.*

MOTHER *(over the intercom, softly)* Who?

SONYA *It's me, Mother, Sonya! Is he home?*

MOTHER *No, Sonya, come on up.*
(hesitates, then rings buzzer)

***SONYA** enters the building, gets into an elevator, goes up and gets out on the right floor, walks to the apartment. The apartment door is ajar, and she goes in.*

ACT THREE

Scene 3

Sonya's parents' apartment

Her MOTHER is standing looking out of a window, her back to SONYA.

SONYA glides in, "Mahogany" style

SONYA	Hi, ma. Don't you have a beautiful daughter?!
(She spins around slowly, smiling)	I'm happy just being alive.

Her smile quickly disappears as her mother turns and faces her.

SONYA	What's wrong, ma? Why so sad?
MOTHER	Sonya, I didn't want to tell you while you were in the hospital, but *(hesitates)* your father is dead.
SONYA *(slight sneer)*	Son of a gun. So the old man croaked.

She looks at a picture of her father, walks over and picks it up

MOTHER *(walks over to SONYA)*	Sonya, he loved you, and he finally came to understand you, but he didn't know how to reach out to you.

SONYA *(disbelief)*	Oh ma. He didn't give a damn about me.
MOTHER *(hangs her head)*	He did, Sonya. He really did.
SONYA *(reaches out, embraces her mother).*	Are you all right?

They separate.

MOTHER	Yes.
SONYA *(softly)*	Mother, I've got to go now, but I'll be back.

SONYA walks out of door to elevator. As elevator door opens, she wipes a tear from her eye.

BACK PROJECTION

SONYA is standing on a corner hailing a cab. She sees a familiar car pass by, but continues to hail her cab. She gets into the cab.

Seated, she leans back, looks out of the rear window, sees the same familiar car following the cab.

SONYA	59th and Lex, please. *(pause)* Wait a minute, *(She reaches her into her purse and takes out a $50 bill and hands it to the cab driver and says)* make that Rural cemetery in White Plains

A few seconds later, she looks again, but the car is gone. She relaxes. The cab pulls up to the cemetery gate, she gets out and walks to her father's grave. The cab waits.

End of Scene 2

ACT THREE

Scene 3

A rural cemetery

***SONYA** is standing at the grave, head bowed, crying softly. She speaks.*

> Father, please forgive me. I've always loved you, and even now I know it's not too late for me to understand that you loved me too.
>
> Look after Mom from up there, and rest in peace.

She slowly turns and takes a few steps, looks over her shoulder and slowly, softly says

> I love you.

She wipes her eyes and walks toward the street.

BACK PROJECTION

When she reaches the cemetery gate, she sees the familiar car again, parked behind the cab. She walks toward it and a window comes down. Still not recognizing the driver, she leans over to see inside. A frightened expression comes upon her face. It's RICHARD.

No dialogue, just picture

WHO ME, YES ME (HEY WORLD) IS BEING SUNG IN THE BACKGROUND

RICHARD *whispers through the window,* "I love you, Sonya."

SONYA *turns and walks away.* RICHARD *gets out of the car and stops her. They talk and gesture.*

SONYA *walks away,* RICHARD *stops her. They talk some more. The* CAB DRIVER *gets out of the cab and gestures, Do you still need me?* SONYA *walks back to the cab, opens the door, looks at* RICHARD, *hesitates, then closes cab door. The* DRIVER *gets back in the cab.*

Seeing this, RICHARD *breaks into a broad smile and runs joyously to* SONYA.

They embrace as the cab pulls away. In the background, the song "Who Me, Yes Me, Hey World" is sung very softly.

SONYA *and* RICHARD *stand for a while, embracing.*

Then they walk arm in arm to Richard's car. As they drive away, they both can be heard singing "HEY WORLD."

The curtain comes down, the lights go out, and DEBBIE is seen standing stage left in front of the curtain.

DEBBIE *completes the song "Hey World"*

The curtain reopens, and the entire cast gathers on stage, singing "Hey World" – an anthem for the worldwide LGBTQ+ Community.

Cast members gesture, interact with one another in recognition and appreciation of their individuality, diversity, shared humanity.

Producers and directors and stage crews join in the song.

They hold hands, bow to the audience, and wave.

THE END

Who Me Yes Me-----------(Hey World)---- Lyrics

Hey World look around---------tell me what do you see.

hey world look around---------change your minds about me.

look into your hearts--------tell me what do you see

a world goin' through changes------that were once------just fantasy

hey world----look at me----I'm just a person------as you can see

accept me being me------and let it be------let it be

I'm not ashamed of what I am-------because God made me this way

two in one------that's how it begun------but now I'm one to stay

hey world------open your hearts------accept what you see in me

you'll say------who is he (she)------I'll say----who me------just me

I live for the day------that I'll hear the world say

you be you------and I'll---------I'll be me

hey world------hey world----look at me------yes me.

Information about sheet music or recordings of the song "HEY WORLD" heard played and sung throughout the play may be obtained through georgesavan724@gmail.com.

The worlds to the song, Hey World, came to me out of the blue, as I was driving down the longest parking lot in the world----(New York's Long Island Express way). I was on my way to work, at one of the loneliest subway stations in the world, Vernon Jackson Ave on the #7 line.

I was feeling really down, because I knew I would have to face another long lonesome night, working in the same Token Booth, where a fellow co-worker, had been senselessly shot (murdered) over a few measly dollars, just three weeks earlier.

As was driving down the LIE, the words came to me like a bolt out of the blue. As I sat in the booth and wrote the words down, I began to hear the melody that would go with the words. The words and the music, stayed in my head, for nearly a month and no matter how I tried to improve on them, they always remained the same.

One day I decided to put the words and music together, on paper and the only person I knew who could that, was (The Minister of Music) at Macedonia AME Church of Flushing Queens, which was officiated by the late great Rev. Dr. Grady Grant Crumpley.

MR. Nathanial Dett Whiting and I met at the church and two hours later, I had a completed project, that I sent off to the Library of Congress the very next day. It was Mr. Whiting's suggestion, that this song could become, the national anthem, for the (LGBTQ) community.

EPILOGUE

In my wildest dreams, I would have never thought that writing this book (play) would have taken me nearly 45 years to complete. But due to circumstances beyond my control and the fact that there was a dispute about who the material belonged to, there was a thin line that caused a lot of controversy.

My partner, Toni, and I were college students at the time we were introduced to the people who lived in The Village area of New York City. These people had a culture of their own that only existed in that area. If you did not live in that small area and were not accepted by them, you most likely would not have been allowed to enter their community, just to collect facts about them, as Toni and I were. We weren't there to hurt them or to laugh at them, and they accepted us because we never lied to them, and we gave them exposure in a positive way, as none of those reporters and researchers who came before us had ever done.

For college students in the mid-1970s, naturally there was a lot of reading to be done. The fact that I had a visual problem made it very difficult for me to keep up with the vast amount of reading material that was required. Enter Professor J. G., my sociology teacher, who made me aware of my problem.

Professor G. suggested that I use the new invention called "Videotape" to actually go out and interview different people who were experiencing different sociological problems. She also suggested that I bring the tapes back and show them to her other students, in a kind of "show and tell," so that all of her students could share what Toni and I had experienced.

Since I had never heard of video, she suggested that I speak to Professor T. P., who was in charge of audio-visual equipment at the LaGuardia Community College.

Professor P. gave me a quick course in video technology and then allowed me to check out video equipment so that we could go out and interview different people of different circumstances. My partner Toni and I started by interviewing veterans who had returned from Vietnam and were attending the college. We branched out and started going to the homes of people who were experiencing financial and sociological problems, such as people on "welfare." We found the reasons for their situations to be both interesting and intriguing, and we learned a great deal about how and why these people's lives had led and were leading them in various directions. We shared our tapes with our fellow students.

With Toni conducting the interviews and me working the equipment, we were able to gather interesting information and take it back to the classroom.

Professor G. was very pleased, because our method allowed her students to see real life situations that they might never have experienced simply by reading a book.

The third person I must pay homage to, and whom I can name, is "Mrs. Satchmo," Louis Armstrong's wife, Lucille Armstrong. We were attending a college that was only two years old. Toni and I had been elected by other students to head up a committee to celebrate Black History Month. As a result, we were able to contact Mrs. Lucille Armstrong, and she agreed to appear at the college and speak about her husband and herself and their roles in Black History.

After meeting with Mrs. Satchmo at her home in the Corona neighborhood in Queens, New York, on two occasions, she decided that she liked both

Toni and me not only as students, but as acquaintances also. We spoke on the phone a number of times, and she even visited my home on two occasions. When she came to the college, we videotaped her appearance and when we showed the video to her and explained that we were going to people's houses and conducting interviews, she suggested that we go to The Village and try to videotape members of the LGBTQ community, because their stories were just as interesting as those of the people we had interviewed previously.

After a year of doing tapes in The Village and showing them in class, we began to gain a reputation for doing videos. We transferred to a four-year college and found that our reputation had preceded us. And as a result, our social studies professor asked us to do more interviews because he wanted to put them on a community access television station that was run by the college.

We eventually got a steady half hour slot on the TV, so we started conducting live interviews with various people from all walks of life, as well as showing our videos of life in The Village.

During the time we were doing our shows, my cousin Clarice, a nurse, introduced me to a doctor who performed sex reassignment surgery. Toni and I met with the doctor and he granted us liberties that would allow us to interview and videotape some of his patients who were both pre- and post-op. We took these tapes back to our college professor, and he put them on the air in the college's closed-circuit system.

They were well received, and we won awards for doing a show that covered the topics we were exploring. Then to my surprise, the doctor asked me if I would videotape the actual sex change operation. He allowed me to videotape five sex change operations over a period of two days.

These tapes of the actual surgeries were not to be shown on television without the written consent of the doctor. However, when we handed in the tapes as a class project, our college professor claimed them as his own personal property and reedited the tapes to make it look as though he had done the interviews.

That action by the professor caused a confrontation that lasted three or four weeks. During that time span, the reedited tapes were sent to the Cannes Film Festival in France by the professor, with the hope of gaining exposure for himself.

This action forced me to get an attorney to file a cease and desist order against the professor, so that the tapes could not be shown, period.

I then had the professor arrested, and he was incarcerated overnight, until he stated that he would return the tapes to the school and give Toni and me the credit that we deserved.

The college had already made up its mind that for having him arrested I should be punished, so I was kicked off the campus for two weeks. After that the doctor and I made a written agreement that the tapes would become his property and that I could not refer to them or do anything involving the sex reassignment surgeries, for twenty years--a twenty-year "gag order."

After twenty years, I realized that this undertaking was still first place in my memory, so I decided that I would try to express what I was feeling by first producing new videotapes of people who had gone through the sex reassignment surgery, exploring how their lives were affected from childhood through adulthood.

Then, I mortgaged my house and tried to produce a movie about the people I had met who had gone through the sex reassignment surgery. Once again, I failed because I did not have enough professional equipment and I did not use professional actors to portray the various roles that were needed. After a year and a half of trying and not being able to complete the movie, I was taken to court by two of the non-professional actors, who sued me for back pay and non-professionalism.

The good news was that I won that particular case and did not have to pay. Winning that particular case only bolstered me to continue to express myself as far as the LGBTQ community was concerned. I still felt that I had a story to tell.

The end result is the book (play) that you have just read or seen, and I hope that it gives every person who reads the book or sees the play some insight into what people of the LGBTQ community have had to experience throughout life and through no fault of their own.

I have had the experience of a lifetime being a fly on the wall, and I hope that through this medium I will be able to share that experience with you.

It is my hope that the song embodied and resonating in this play, "HEY WORLD!...Who Me – yes Me" might become a theme song for the entire LGBTQ+ community as each person struggles to affirm and become his/her/their own "Me." It is also a song for everyone in the human community who is engaged in our common struggle to become who we are, overcoming brutality of every kind.

Special thanks to

My partner Toni, my cousin Clarice, my teachers, all who have encouraged my work. Our debt to the courageous identity-affirmers in this story and all those who helped and continue to help them sing "Who Me? Yes Me!" is beyond adequate expression.

In these recent years and months, Lilyanne Whiteson, Roy and Marilyn Magers, Natalie Madison, Margie Salters, Charmaine Colthirst, Dallas Crumpley, Jacqueline Seawright, Rodney Seawright, and Danielle Keith-Seawright have helped, patiently, to bring this work toward its completion.

You all know what you have done!

WHO ME ...YES ME   J L SEAWRIGHT

Lightning Source UK Ltd.
Milton Keynes UK
UKHW011011210820
368606UK00001B/160